Talent-Show Pups

By Sierra Harimann
Illustrated by The Artifact Group

SCHOLASTIC INC.

ISBN 978-0-545-47234-0

12 11 10 9 8 7 6 5 4 3 2 1   13 14 15 16 17 18/0

Designed by Angela Jun

Printed in the U.S.A.   40

This edition first printing, February 2013

Gigi's alarm went off bright and early. She leaped out of bed and pulled on her tutu.

"First position, point, second position, *plié*, and together!" Gigi chanted as she practiced.

Gigi twirled into the kitchen. Freddy and Montana were there eating breakfast.

"*Bonjour!*" said Gigi.

"You have a lot of energy this morning," Montana told her friend as she rubbed her eyes sleepily.

"*Mmmm,*" Freddy mumbled in agreement.

"I'm practicing for the Puppyville Talent Show!" Gigi exclaimed. "It's only a few weeks away."

"Thanks for the reminder, Gigi," Montana replied. "I have to brush up on my juggling skills."

She grabbed three oranges from a bowl and began tossing them in the air.

"Wow," cried Freddy. "I didn't know you could juggle, Montana. You're good!"

Montana blushed. "Thanks, Freddy," she said. "I taught myself a few months ago, but I still have to practice a lot. I don't want to drop something in the middle of the talent show!"

"Did someone say 'talent show'?" Spike barked as he entered the kitchen. "I've got a comedy routine all ready to go."

Clarissa and Fuji were close behind him.

"Boy, everyone's up early today," Clarissa said.

"We're all talking about the Puppyville Talent Show," Freddy told her. "Are you going to perform, too?"

"Yes," Clarissa replied, gesturing toward Fuji. "I'm going to sing while Fuji plays the piano."

"I wish I had a talent to show off," Freddy said sadly. "But even if I did, I think I'd be too shy to get up on stage alone in front of all those puppies."

"Well, we still need a producer for the show, Freddy," Montana told her friend. "I think you'd be great at it. What do you say?"

"Me?" Freddy asked, surprised. "You really think I could produce the entire show?"

"Of course!" Montana replied confidently. "You'd be the best."

"I'll do it, then!" Freddy barked with excitement.

The next week, the puppies rehearsed every day. Freddy watched each puppy practice his or her act, and he decided on the lineup for the show. He also made a list of all the extra materials and equipment the puppies would need.

The day before the show, they held a dress rehearsal.

"Attention, pups," Freddy announced. "Let's try running through the show from beginning to end. Ivy is going to be the announcer, so listen for her to call your name."

The dress rehearsal was a success. Everything went smoothly.

"Great job, puppies!" Freddy told them. "Get a good night's rest so we can put on a fantastic show tomorrow."

The next evening, Freddy was the first one to arrive at the theater. Gigi burst in looking upset.

"Freddy!" Gigi cried. "I need your help! I can't find the CD with my dance music."

"Relax, Gigi," Freddy said calmly. "We'll figure something out. What was the name of your song again?"

"It's 'Clair de Lune'," Gigi said through sniffles.

At that moment, Clarissa and Fuji arrived backstage.

"Fuji," Freddy said. "Just the puppy I wanted to talk to! Can you play 'Clair de Lune' on the piano?"

"Of course," Fuji barked. "That's one of my favorites."

"Terrific!" Freddy replied. "Would you mind playing the song during Gigi's ballet routine?"

"Not at all," Fuji said.

"Oh, merci!" Gigi cried, giving Fuji a hug. "Thank you so much! Let's practice it once before the other puppies arrive."

"That's a great idea," Clarissa agreed. "Fuji and I had plenty of time to practice this week. I'll just change into my costume while you two rehearse."

Clarissa pulled her dress out of her bag.

RIP!

The dress caught on the bag's zipper and tore.

"My dress!" Clarissa exclaimed. "It's ruined."

"Can I take a look at it?" Freddy asked.

Clarissa handed the dress to him.

"This will be easy to fix," Freddy said. "See? It's ripped along the seam, which I can sew up easily. Leave it to me."

"Wow, Freddy," Clarissa replied, giving Freddy a hug. "You're the best! Thanks!"

Freddy blushed.

"It's no problem," he said.

Freddy was fixing Clarissa's dress when Montana arrived. She began unpacking her things.

"I don't understand," Montana barked in frustration. "I know I packed my juggling bean bags, but they aren't here. And I don't have enough time to go home to get them before the show starts."

She hung her head sadly.

"I have an idea," Freddy said. "Remember when you juggled for me in the kitchen last week? You used three oranges."

Montana nodded.

"Well, you can juggle fruit!" Freddy continued. "I packed an apple and an orange for a snack, and I'm sure we can find at least one other round thing."

21

Freddy looked through a box of props.

"Yes!" he exclaimed as he pulled out a baseball. "This will be perfect."

"Thanks, Freddy," Montana barked. "What would I have done without you?"

A short while later, the show was about to start. The audience was packed, and everyone was lined up backstage.

"Break a paw, puppies!" Ivy told them before she stepped onto the stage to announce the first act.

The show was going smoothly. Spike's comedy routine was the next act.

He stepped onto the stage and cleared his throat.

"What did the Labrador puppy wear in chemistry class?"

Suddenly, Spike froze. He had stage fright! He couldn't remember the rest of the joke. But Freddy remembered it from rehearsal and whispered it from backstage.

Spike heard Freddy and, in an instant, remembered his entire routine.

"A lab coat!" He barked out the punch line happily. The puppies in the audience all laughed.

The rest of the show was a huge success.

"Thank you all for coming to the Puppyville Talent Show!" Ivy announced after the final act. "And now I have a very special award to present: the trophy for 'Most Talented Puppy'! And the award goes to . . . "

"... Freddy!"

Freddy was stunned. He stepped out onto the stage for the first time that night.

"But I didn't even do anything!" Freddy said.

"Yes, you did!" Montana corrected him. "You were the world's most talented producer. We couldn't have done it without you."

"She's right," Spike agreed. "You saved my act. . . . "

"And the show!" Gigi added.

Montana and Clarissa nodded in agreement.

"Thank you," Freddy said as he accepted the trophy. "I dedicate this award to the most talented puppies in Puppyville . . . my friends!"